Got W.I.P.D.?

The Recipe for a Successful Marriage

Hansen Anthony Harper

Table
of Ingredients

Foreword

It has been one of my best blessings to have walked with Hansen Harper as a friend, a mentor and brother in Christ for many years now. His candid and engaging style is a gift from the Kingdom of God, as you will well know once you get a few pages into this book. *Got W.I.P.D.?* will reveal the hairline cracks that led an excited pair of newlyweds toward a major meltdown and ultimate disaster in their once sacred relationship. With humor, heartbreak and humility, Hansen delivers his own unique story of how God intervened at precisely the right time to heal and mature him and his wife as they found themselves floundering through the tense and often bitter struggles that plague so many marriages in our country. Most of those marriages, unfortunately, end up in divorce court.

With great courage and determination, Hansen and Dionne turned the tide and ran to the only one they knew could save them, individually and as a couple. With God's intervention, they learned to search themselves rather than passing judgment on each other. Step by step, God showed them how to rekindle and renew the bonds of holy matrimony that seemed at one time shredded beyond repair. Having walked this story as a couple, the Lord laid it on Hansen's heart to share the ingredients they discovered along the way. From the heartfelt discussions at the kitchen table, to the transparent and humorous insights he shares with the reader, you will come away from each chapter knowing that there is hope for your marriage, no matter what condition it is in at the moment. Even seasoned married couples will come away inspired to rejuvenate areas of their relationship that become neglected as life goes by.

Got W.I.P.D.? is a Godsend to all married couples in these seemingly godless times. It is more than a marriage repair manual. Packed with keen biblical insights, it conveys a strategy that all couples can build on to find and live the blessings that God intended for us to enjoy through the lifetime commitment that He ordained in the marriage covenant. Not many couples survive marriage these days. Even Christian couples can wind up devastated and emotionally crippled through divorce. By adding one ingredient at a time, we can find ourselves experiencing the holy, harmonious and happy matrimony that God intended to bless us with.

Henry Abraham
Founder and CEO of Christ Centered Man International
www.CCMan365.com

Acknowledgments

I want to first thank my Lord and savior Jesus Christ for saving me from a life of hell and definite destruction. He made me come to myself and realize that it is not me who lives, but Him through me. I would like to thank my father and mother Floyd and Ovellia Harper for always encouraging me to do my best. They believed and supported me when I did not believe and could not support myself, and for that I am eternally grateful.

I want to thank my mentor and founder of Christ Centered Man International, Henry Abraham, who obeyed God and told me that I should write a book in 2009. Then he told me again in December 2012. This time I listened. Minister Abraham has spent countless hours helping me on understanding the in's and out's of writing a book. Through his patience, guidance, and dedication you are reading something that was actually just a thought 4 years ago today.

I would like to thank my grandparents, Willie and Pearlie Seltz, who are the epitome of what a God-centered marriage is. They have been together for 64 years! Talk about commitment!!! Thanks to Johnivan Darby for assisting in the editing process. Thanks to world-renowned photographer, Nuru Kimondo, for her expertise and gorgeous photos.

Thank you to my lovely wife Dionne, who puts up with the Hansen that no one sees and supports me through the thick and thin. To my kids, Zion and Zoe, I am so glad that I GOT WIP'd because you guys bring nothing but joy to me everyday and I am blessed for having you. I would like to thank my mother-in-law Ruby Douglas for helping edit this book and advising me to take my time writing it. I would like to thank all of the students that I have ever taught at Thea Bowman Leadership Academy. To all the pastors who ever taught me: Victor Davis, James Middleton, Sam Douglas, Roosevelt Bradley Jr, and Greg Howse, thank you all so much for your spiritual guidance in the ways and thoughts of our Lord Jesus Christ. I hope I am not forgetting anyone. To all my family and friends, thank you for your inspiration, and remember, I love you all in Jesus' name.

Dedication

This book is dedicated to my grandmother, Pearlie M. Seltz (August 11th, 1930-October 6th, 2013), who is currently present with our Lord and Savior Jesus Christ. I honor her in death as I honored her in life for her kindness, devotion, and endless support of God, husband, children, grandchildren and her church. There is not one person who has ever encountered my grandmother who has not felt the love and overwhelming grace of Jesus Christ. May others feel the same love and overwhelming grace of Jesus through me that I may ultimately offer Christ to them. Stop spanking the angels Grandma. They don't have to wash their hands before dinner! I love you!

-Hansen

Preface

Thank you for picking up a tool that will change your marriage forever. I really want you and your spouse to get together and get the meat out of what I am trying to convey through this book. Are you single? Even better! This book is designed to fix your relationship no matter what stage it may be. I want you to know that you can have the victory and peace in a God-centered marriage.

Just a little about me. I really did not have that great of a dating experience but as I later found out, I was searching in all the wrong places for the right things. *Got W.I.P.D.?* tells my journey from a pretty decent childhood, all the way up to my current 8 years of being married to the same beautiful woman, Dionne Harper. I hail from meager beginnings in a small town called Gary, Indiana. I attended Indiana University where I attained my Bachelors degree. Raised in the fear and admonishment of God by my parents Floyd and Ovellia Harper, the call of God was always on my life. Even as a youngster I kept asking so many questions that people would literally tell me to be quiet. But I always knew in the back of my head that God was going to use me to do something great.

This book is a really powerful tool for singles, engaged, and married couples to sit down and have a group discussion about how God takes all the ups and downs in our lives and blends them into something we could never have imagined on our own. At the end of each chapter of *Got W.I.P.D.?* there is a "Kitchen Table Discussions" section for you to utilize. I added this piece because I remember as a young man in my father's house, no matter what time of day or night, we would discuss all of our problems around the kitchen table. It was a place of good news, bad news, and all the in between. No matter what, you were going to leave with solutions to your problems.

Like those "Kitchen Table Discussions," I want this text to be God's solution to healing your relationship. I promised God that if there was anyway that I could save some single person from feeling that they are never going to get married, or some couple on the brink of breaking up / divorce, that the struggles that went along with writing this book would be all worth it. I want God to guide, heal, and restore relationships through this book. God has truly used my gift of communication to mentor and train singles and married couples on how to build and maintain a God-centered relationship. In conclusion, it is our hope and prayer that you apply the principles contained in this book to see how my wife and I both Got W.I.P.D.!

Ingredient 1

Silence Papers

Mark 9:42
"But whoever causes one of these little ones who believe in me to sin, it would be better for him to have a great millstone fastened around his neck and to be drowned in the depth of the sea."

I was given an assignment while attending Indiana University that altered my life from that day on. I was to remember a time in my existence where someone "silenced" me. All of us have experienced "silencing" in a bad marriage, overbearing parents, being victims of physical, verbal, or sexual abuse. "Silencing" happens when someone in a position of power violates and abuses the trust you have for them by limiting your progress, whether physically, mentally, or spiritually. What I am about to share with you is not easy at all for me because it takes me back to a dark place in my life where I was literally helpless.

My name is Hansen Anthony Harper. I vividly remember a cold and dark night in December; there was snow outside and all I wanted to do was play. At the time, I was about 7 and my sister 8, my parents were a part of this Christian Women's movement or something similar. That night, my parents, along with my aunt and uncle, were supposed to go to a dinner. My parents then told my sister and I that we would be getting baby-sat over my favorite cousin's house. That was fine with us as long as she was going to be there. We knew we were going to have fun! As soon as we arrived there, I noticed that our favorite cousin was not there. I immediately begged my dad to take my sister and I with them because they had done it before. I remember him and my mom really considering it, but for whatever reason, they decided to leave us at our uncle's house with our older cousins whom we really did not know. That was when I felt the pits of hell burning under my feet. Something was just not right!

My sister and I never really had a great relationship with my 3 older cousins who just happened to be at the house and were available to baby-sit. I guess they were all right, but we never really talked to them because they were older. The oldest girl cousin was upstairs on the phone. I distinctly remember knocking on her door and asking her to let us in so we could play with her, but she would not let us in. You know how teenage girls are; she was on the phone, probably talking to her boyfriend or something. Anyway, my sister and I sat there in the living room trying to entertain each other when we heard this male voice say nicely to us, "Y'all come on downstairs." Listening to him was a decision we both would live to regret.

At my cousin's house, downstairs always felt dark, cold, and scary. This night's experience became all those things and more for us; it would change our lives forever. My older male cousin, we shall call him "Ray", told my sister and I to come down the stairs. All the lights were off and I remember the only thing I could see was this weird remote control robot that Ray was playing with and also trying to scare us with. It was totally black down the stairs. All we could see was this robot's red eyes beaming up and down at the bottom of the stairs. My sister and I ended up running back up. This is where Ray got more demanding, "Y'all come back down here before y'all get a spanking!" Our parents taught us that if an adult asks you to do something, you were supposed to do it. All of a sudden my sister went obediently down the stairs and faded into the darkness. I yelled for her to come back up the stairs, but she had already disappeared into the darkness.

Although my sister is a year older than me, I always felt like I was her protector, so I could not leave her down there by herself. Valiantly into the dark, damp, and evil basement I went. I didn't know what would be my fate, but when I reached the bottom of the stairs, it was pitch black. I knew something was not right. Ray then commanded my sister and I to go to the bathroom…with him in it. Even at 7 years old I knew this was not right, but we went in obedience. That night Ray, our older teenage cousin, violated both of us and told us that we better not tell anyone.

I really don't remember much after that, but as soon as my parents came back and I knew that I was safely in my dad's car, I TOLD! I TOLD!! I TOLD!!! "Dad! Ray messed with us downstairs!" We explained explicitly what he did to us. My father kept asking questions to see if we were sure, and my Dad knew that what I was describing could not have been imagined. So many questions were running through my head. Could I have done something to prevent this? Should I have just grabbed my sister ran out of the house? Should I have fought back? Ray, why did you do it? Dad, why didn't you just take us with you? I don't understand. Even right now, it's really painful to talk about because it brings up so many bad feelings. When I told Dad, I thought things would be better. However, this would become a demon I would struggle with my whole life.

Lessons I Learned

Have you ever witnessed someone try to hold their breath for an extended period of time? Eventually they have to let the air out. That is what I am doing right now...LETTING IT OUT! Wherever you are right now, and whoever you are with, just Let it OUT. You will see how much better you feel. While typing up the story of Ray, I was in tears because I thought I was over it but I am not. The ONLY reason I am revealing this part of my journey is because God said writing about this would help somebody, and if you're that somebody, I hope this helps. My sister and I were victims of child abuse at 7 and 8 years old, and even as a grown man, it sometimes finds its way back into my memory. I finally realize now that there was nothing that I could have possibly done because this was a grown man and he was my elder. I personally have never been to counseling, but I will be attending very soon.

This has come to be a very bad trend in the minority community as far as not speaking out about people in your family or in the church that are child predators. The truth is, if you expose that person, that is one less victim that is freed from the hands of a pedophile. Don't be mistaken. The devil will even use family members to distort the lives of an innocent child. I am older now, and I have seen Ray around here and there. I say hello and that's about it. One thing about predators, they are the ultimate cowards. They take advantage of the weak to make themselves feel strong, never realizing that they leave lifetime scars.

I have often asked God, "Why did you let this happen to me?" I personally believe God's answer to me was that this was part of my process. In my future relationships, this abuse experience created feelings of low self-esteem and being overprotective of anything that was mine. Though traumatizing, I would not be the man I am now. It did not stop me. Don't let it stop you! Let it OUT!

Kitchen Table Reflections

1. Have you ever been, or know someone who has been abused as a child? How has that affected your/their feelings regarding relationships?

2. If you have experienced abuse in the past, have you and/or your spouse sought any professional counseling? If not, when will you?

3. How would "Letting it Out" (telling your story to others), make you feel?

4. Why don't more families warn other family members about the abusers in their own families?

Ingredient 2

No Hope for Me

Isaiah 40:30-31
"Even youths grow tired and weary, and young men stumble and fall; but those who hope in the Lord will renew their strength. They will soar on wings like eagles; they will run and not grow weary, they will walk and not be faint."

Now let's fast forward 21 years.

This is really ridiculous! I am a 28 year old grown man, and I still have not gotten married. I have been raised in the church my whole life and by this time next year, if I do not get married, I am just going to become a monk! Oh, believe me, it's not because I couldn't start a relationship with a young lady, but it seemed that every woman I dated had something extremely wrong with them.

I know you must think I'm joking. One young lady on the 1st date admitted to me that she was divorced. This babe was fine. However, I had a feeling in my heart that she was not finished unloading all of her garbage on me. After that, she told me that she had something else to tell me. In the back of my mind I am thinking, "God please don't let this be a man in my car," but calmly and slowly she told me that she just got out of jail. HOLD UP!!! By now, I've got one hand on the steering wheel, one hand on the door handle, and my foot is almost fully extended on the gas. Trying to stay cool without looking or sounding like a wimp, I mustered up the courage to ask her what she was in jail for. Why did I ask this ignorant, yet honest question? What she said next was one of the most startling things I had ever heard in my life and completely unexpected. Her head snapped sharply to the left and she stared me dead in my eyes and said with no hesitation, "I murdered my husband!"

"WHAT!" From that second on, my mind went blank and I remember praying to God, "Lord, don't let this lady zone out in her mind and reenact the scene of her killing her husband with me!" I dropped her off at her house so fast! And she even had the nerve to ask me if I was I going to walk her to her door. I didn't even dignify that with a response. I WAS OUT!!! Pretty funny huh? Go ahead and get your laughs out. Looking back at it now I can laugh about it, too. But believe me, my relationships in the future would only get more and more problematic.

My next relationship was with a young lady who was a holy roller. She could not do anything! She could not even go to the bowling alley for fear that it was full of the devil. To make it even worse, her mother disliked me because I was not saved. Her mom's idea of being saved was being able to speak in tongues on cue. If one of the members of the church asked you to prove you were saved, you had to start speaking in tongues. So myself, being young and stupid, I joined this particular church because maybe my relationship with God was not as tight as I thought it was. Besides all of that, she was fine!

One day, this young lady and I got into a heated argument about the Holy Ghost. She and her church believed that to receive the Holy Ghost you had to tarry (wait) at church for it. When you got it, you would start speaking in an unknown tongue. I then informed her that you don't have to pray for the

17

Holy Ghost just to speak in tongues because as soon as you accept Jesus into your heart, the Holy Ghost already dwells within you. The tongues are just one of the byproducts of having the holy spirit in you. To add, the fruits of the spirit according to Galatians 5:22-23 in the Bible are love, joy, peace, patience, kindness, goodness, faithfulness, and self-control. By the end of the debate, she had still convinced me that I needed the Holy Ghost so I could speak in tongues. Hey, I told you she was fine.

It was a Wednesday night and I went into the "tarrying" room. This was a room specifically in this young lady's church where people seeking the Holy Ghost with the evidence of speaking in tongues went to. Needless to say, I had no idea of what I was getting into. One of the ladies in the room told me to just start saying "Jesus, Jesus" over and over as fast as I could! After about twenty minutes of this fiasco, and with a mouth as dry as a piece of firewood, I slowed down and thought about just walking out. Then out of the corner of my eyes I saw these two young kids, probably about seven or eight on their knees praying for the Holy Ghost. They were balling their eyes out and saying Jesus so hard, I felt bad for slacking off. All of a sudden, an older lady who was over this tarrying boot camp yelled to these two young kids, "All right, you guys get up right now! You all are not serious about getting the Holy Ghost tonight. You all are just playing around. Come back next week!"

I am telling you; you would have been appalled at the treatment of these children. Their Bambi eyes opened wide as if they were in total shock. They pleaded with the lady earnestly to let them keep trying. The lady did not want to hear it. The tarrying drill sergeant kicked them out of the room. Needless to say, after that night, I was through with the young lady, that church, and her idea of being saved! Not to mention the fact that during this time, she had some type of prophetic message saying that God told her to break up with me. I kept on trying to reason with her. We would get back together, and things would get worse and worse. After about the 5th time of this young lady's revelations, we broke up with each other. To this day, we have still never spoken.

Feeling bad for me yet? Well don't. Like the old church folks used to say, some trials you go through in life are a blessing in disguise: a blessing that they came, and a blessing that they're gone! If I would tell you all the rest of my dating exploits, it would take up too much time. You are definitely getting the picture now about my dating picks. With my luck, I thought I was probably going to be one of those old men in the park playing chess and feeding the pigeons crumbled bread. I felt that I was like a lamb unguided in this dating game, and I had nothing to show for it. At least a lamb has its wool. What did I have? I did all I could do. I really didn't know what more to do. I was confused, concerned, and consequently, an unmarried Christian.

Lessons I Learned

I have found out that it is not necessary to know all the details about our lives. God is so loving that He gives us life in pieces. I remember as a boy in church, my mother would take a peppermint and would crack it in pieces with her teeth. She would then give me just a little bit of that peppermint a piece at a time. Quite naturally as a 5 year old boy, I'm like, "Is this lady crazy? Give it all to me now!" However, my wise mother knew that I could not handle it because several times previously I had been playing with a whole peppermint in my mouth and almost choked. Was there anything wrong with the peppermint? No. It was good for me, but my mother gave me what she knew I could handle so I would not choke. Just like life, we are in such a hurry for that job, that money, that man or woman, but God continues to tell us through circumstances and conditions that, "Hey Son/Daughter, this is all you can handle." When God thinks you are ready for more He will give you more.

Believe me, I know the game out there has slim pickings, but I made a drastic commitment to God as a young man. I promised him that I would just seek him and not date for about a year. About 8 months later, Dionne (my wife) came along. If you want something from God, you must seek him first (Matthew 6:33). When God is honored with your sacrifice, He will provide you with a tangible reward. At that time when I was single, I searched for a mate more than God. For both male and female, this is not what God wants from you. God is a jealous God and will have no other before him (Exodus 20:5). If you are single, try fasting from dating for at least 8 months. I am not saying that it is going to be easy, but if you stick with it, you will be successful (Read Jeremiah 29:11). Dedicate your mind, soul, and body to Christ. Act as if you were dating God daily, and I promise, it won't be too long before that significant other comes calling. Come on! Just seriously try it and I know you will be so glad that you did. (Read Matthew 6:33).

Kitchen Table Reflections

1. Can you see a positive/negative pattern in the type of people you have chosen to have relationships with in the past? How have they helped/hurt you?

2. In your opinion, do Christian singles tend to just tolerate the opposite sex during the dating process even if he/she knows that they are wrong for each other? Read and discuss 2 Corinthians 6:14-18.

3. What's the best way to prepare yourself for marriage?

4. Can you see your life, marriage, and relationship through the lens of the peppermint story? How?

Ingredient 3

The Internet Beauty

Matthew 7:7
"Ask, and it will be given to you; seek, and you will find; knock, and it will be opened to you."

I'm just getting off work and I've been wondering; the life of a single Christian person sure is lonely. Do you hear what I'm saying singles? I mean, I wake up by myself, go to bed by myself, and eat by myself. Every once in a while, my friends, D and Rodney, get together for a knockdown, drag out Playstation marathon of NBA Live. Other than that, I am a lonely man.

I do, however, have a young married couple that I highly respect at the church called Gerald and Dianne. I came across G about two years ago. He was new to the Christian faith. The thing I was most impressed with about him was how he treated his wife. I said to myself, "That's what I want!" So I stayed hanging out with G and his family, and they never turned me away. G was like the older brother that I never had and, of course, I trusted him. G, being about 8 years older than me, kept on reminding me to wait on God for a wife and that in His time He would send the perfect one for me. "That's what all married people say," I thought and left it alone. After leaving G's and getting back to my own house, I often broke down in tears and shouted, "God is there something wrong with me?!"

Even all the extra ugly guys have gorgeous women. OK God, I know that I have been very picky in the past, but I'll even accept an ugly woman at this point! Hold on God…just don't let her be too ugly. OK Lord, even if she has one, just one missing tooth, I can deal with that. But seriously God, just let the missing tooth be toward the back of her smile and not right in front.

"All right, stop thinking, you're sounding real desperate," I thought to myself. I spent that entire night bargaining with God for my future companion. The next day, it was off to G's as usual. When I finally arrived, I was at my breaking point. I had stayed up all night and I thought the next day at least, one of my requests to God would be answered. I felt worse than ever before. I remember just breaking down to my friend G and letting him know that I felt like I was at my lowest. He mentioned three words that dramatically changed my life, "Try the Internet!"

"What? Now wait a minute! Do you think I am that desperate? No, forget about it. This is 2001! Church people don't find dates on the Internet! I might as well be paying a prostitute or something. No, forget about it. That's downright disgusting. You mean possibly getting in contact with a serial killer? No way! I've had my share of nutcases. You must be out of your…"

"OK. I'll try it G, just this once. But if it doesn't work out, I am telling you, the monastery option is looking better and better." I timidly and cautiously tried a very popular online dating site. Now you must remember, in the early 2000s, online dating was still taboo for most church going people. At this point, all of my other options were depleted. Will I meet the love of my life or Susan the Psycho? We'll see. Needless to say, I paid my start up fee and it was very easy and non-confrontational how this online service had it's system hooked up. They go through a series of deep questions of likes and dislikes that forced me to be honest with others and myself. Now I've done it; I have launched myself off into the cyberspace dating game. I promised myself that I would only try this service for a month and if it did not work, then I would sign up for the monastery. I told God, "Don't be ashamed of me. This is just, well, you know God, I'm just desperate."

Lessons I Learned

Though I was not fond of searching for a wife on the Internet, I got on that website and searched for my wife. Don't wait for a potential wife to chase you; you chase her. Be Godly and aggressive. After all, God did promise: He who findeth a wife, findeth a good thing and receiveth favor from the Lord (Proverbs 18:22). Men, go seek your wife! It's OK. Women, be ready too! While your husband is searching for you, don't make it so hard to be found! Act, dress, and imagine that every day is going to be the day that "the one" is going to find you. Ladies, you can do it! (Read Matthew 25:1-13)

Kitchen Table Reflections

1. As a Christian, should you consider Internet dating at all?
   Why or why not?

2. Why does being single seem to be so hard at times especially when
   you see other married couples happy and together?

3. Every couple needs a mentor couple. Who is/will be your mentor
   couple? (Please take a few minutes to discuss this.) Write down
   three reasons why you picked this particular couple to mentor you?

4. What is the weirdest thing you have ever tried to do to find the
   right mate? (If it involves something illegal, please keep it to
   yourself.)

Ingredient 4

I Found Her

Philippians 4:6
"Do not be anxious about anything, but in everything, by prayer and petition, with thanksgiving, present your requests to God."

All right God. I have been on, in and around this Internet dating site for about 28 days. I've just been spinning my wheels. I have just two more days left on my trial period. If I don't hit the jackpot, I'm through with the whole possibility of dating or marriage at all. I had a couple of leads, which were pretty interesting, while I was on the Internet. One young lady lived on a farm in Natchez, Mississippi. Natchez, Mississippi? I had never heard of that place before and she didn't make me want to visit. I like to talk, but this young lady talked a little bit too much. That was not cool with me. I couldn't get a word in edgewise in any of our conversations. To probably our mutual delight, one day she stopped emailing and so did I. Feeling at my lowest point, a young lady from Calumet City, IL popped up on my screen. I am always shopping at the mall over there and Calumet City was less than 15 miles away from my house. This thing may work, so we began to have a conversation about Mel Gibson's Passion of the Christ movie.

There was something different about this young lady's conversation that really sparked my interest. She was a couple years older than me, loved God, and sounded halfway intelligent. The major problem was that I only had one more day of eligibility left on this very popular dating site. From the beginning, I promised myself that I wasn't going to spend any more money on this dating site. Since this young lady and I had not gotten to the final stage in the website match up, which means exchanging numbers and addresses, I decided to speed things up just a little. I emailed her my phone number to get in contact with me directly. Furthermore, I told her that if she was really serious about meeting up, then she should call me. If not, that was going to be my last day on this website. Well people, I had given it my best shot. In my mind, I had gone to the lowest place I could possibly go to find a suitable mate. Maybe she will call, and maybe she won't. Oh well, Holy Angels Monastery is looking better and better with each passing minute. I wonder what color robe I would look best in?

Later that evening, the guys and I were playing our usual all night Playstation game and I ended up getting the weirdest phone call. I picked up the phone and the voice said, "Hello. May I speak to Hansen?" Of course thinking it was a bill collector I asked, "Who's asking?" The voice then sweetened and said so gently, "This is Dionne." My heart skipped one million beats! But of course, I had to play it cool because my boys were around. I replied in the deepest and smoothest voice that I could muster, "Oh, hey. You decided to call huh?" Now that I think about it, that line was not smooth at all. Romeo would have never talked to Juliet that way. Anyway, from that day on I was 100% sure that I would officially no longer be considering the priesthood ever again. IT WAS A MATCH! But for how long? I had yet to see. As I went to bed, I gave God his props and said to God, "You are pretty clever, but I've got my eyes on you. I am watching your every move on this deal. Don't leave me hanging…Please."

Lessons I Learned

Man, God hooked me up! I'm telling you. I was not going to spend another dime on that website. It just goes to show you, God will use the strangest ways to bless you. When God hooks you up, make sure to give him praise and thanks. The Lord delights in the praises of his people. The key is not to just praise him when all is going well. Praise the Lord when things seem like they won't get any better (Read Psalms 22:3). I am still not totally sold on Internet dating, though I found my beautiful wife on it. Pray and ask God for the avenue that he wants you to actually go seek your wife/wait for your husband. OK?

Kitchen Table Reflections

1. Has God ever answered your prayer concerning someone you thought had potential to be "the one" just in the nick of time? I mean something only you and God knew about?

2. What is the importance of conversation while getting to know someone during the dating process?

3. Did/do you think you would/will ever find the right person to marry and spend life happily ever after? Why or why not?

Ingredient 5

Full Speed Ahead

Ecclesiastes 11:9
"Rejoice, O young man, in your youth, and let your heart cheer you in the days of your youth; walk in the ways of your heart, and in the sight of your eyes; but know that for all these God will bring you into judgment."

From the start we hit it off! We were laughing, joking, going out, and talking on the phone all night. It was amazing! Dionne was not like anyone I had ever met. She was tall, beautiful, intelligent, and her eyes were so big, it was as if she was staring right into my soul. We did everything, everyday, and all the time; we were inseparable. I remember entering a drawing for a Chicago White Sox Party package for 2 and I won! I mean this was big! And it gets better than that; Dionne and I were even picked up in a limousine courtesy of this party package, dinner at Mike Ditka's in Chicago…all on the house! Man, this was crazy; I got my girl, the game, and a limo ride. Can you say, "The Man?" I was on top of the world! And to think, all this time I had been mixing and mingling through the trash can called "dating" to finally find something that was all for me. Stevie Wonder's song said it best. "For Once in my Life" was playing over and over again in my head. Pinch me; I must be dreaming! God, you are pretty cool. I knew I wasn't that bad of a Christian. I am on my A-game and nothing can stop me now.

Of course by now, the guys think I am shady because I'm not staying up until 3 a.m. with them battling it out on Playstation. My family is still checking Dionne out. "There are definitely things you don't know about each other," said my Dad. Well, tough luck to all of you guys! At this point, I could really care less what they think because I am with my baby. Do you know how hard it has been for me to get a decent woman? Up until this point I have had to deal with holy rollers, nutcases, psychopaths, mama's girls, sleep around Sallys, one night Wendys, all night Nancys, too young Tinas, still married Susies, and too old Olivias? I feel like I have been running a marathon, dehydrated for 28 years, and suddenly ice-cold bottled water appears out of nowhere. Yep! I am going to drink until I can't drink anymore!

Unfortunately, that has been my biggest downfall with Dionne, my new-found love. What we are about to willingly participate in will produce one of the biggest trials/blessing I have ever had in my life. Just being honest, my bride to be and I drank heavily from the bottle of pre-marital sex and we had no plans of getting full. We were a church boy and a church girl who knew better, but we were also young, able, and ignorant. We yelled "AMEN" in church, but at night we fueled our lustful desires with a temporary sense of satisfaction from the fruit basket of sin. We were wrong, and we knew it! We liked it, and we wanted more. We chose to ignore the signs that God naturally put up to protect or warn his children when they are in danger. Come on! You know those subtle signs. For instance, while we were engulfed in sinful exercise, a TV evangelist would pop on the screen speaking about Jesus. At other times one of our family members would call and start asking us a lot of questions. I vividly remember one day. My pastor at the time drove up in his car to my house just after we finished a day of passion "just to check on me." What is it about sin that does not want to be found out? The pastor did not say much else after that, but I think he knew that we were not right. How I wished I had listened to God's several warnings. As a consequence of my outright disobedience, our relationship (Dionne and I) was getting ready to spiral into another dimension. We had the chance to stop but we did not. It's funny how when I think back to that time, the Lord was still looking out for us. Here comes the boom…

One night I had the guys over and we were playing an all out NBA Live 2005 extravaganza all night as we did very often. At that very moment, I felt some type of uneasiness. All of a sudden, I got a phone call. It was Dionne. I said hello and the first thing she said was, "I've got to tell you something." I got a strange feeling like déjà vu. What was about to come out of her mouth would change the course of both of our lives forever. The guys were all into the game and I wanted to tell them to just go home but those were my boys, my compadres, so I played it cool like everything was all good. I backed back by the bathroom and asked Dionne what she was talking about. She repeated again that she had something to tell me. In my mind I was praying, "Please don't let this girl tell me she has a husband, a disease, kids, a jail record, is a convicted killer, or wants to break up with me because God said so. Lord I can't handle much more." "Well, what do you have to tell me?" I asked. She replied, "I AM PREGNANT!"

My heart dropped under the earth! "You're what?" I shouted. By that time, my boys had turned around because I was shouting, and I couldn't tell them what was really going on. I told them that Dionne had got into a bad accident and that I had to go see her right away. All the guys rushed out of the house as I shook in my boots. "Dionne, are you playing, or are you serious? You're playing, right?" I asked. Dionne said, "No. I am serious. I am pregnant!" Man oh man, how could this have happened to me? No, she has got to be lying, "Who else have you been sleeping with?" I uttered out. All hell broke loose. What are we going to do?

I don't even remember how I got over to her house that night. As soon as I got there I rushed out of the car as if I was late to catch the train. When I saw her, we both fell in each other's arms and just broke down crying! What are we going to do? From that point on, we both were forced to do a whole lot of growing up and making some very tough decisions. Why me Lord?

Lessons I Learned

I know, I know. Sex feels so good, but guess what? Outside of marriage, it is so wrong! I knew it just like you know it now. But at that time, I felt like I should indulge myself because I had been waiting so patiently and so long. But God's word is still God's word (Read Galatians 6:7-8). God already knows what's up. Everything we do, we do it before the eyes of the Lord. The Bible also says that obedience is better than sacrifice (1 Samuel 15:22). If you are obedient, you will not have to sacrifice. I was wrong guys, but the good thing is that God's grace and mercy still abounds. Turn off the TV and get off of the Internet! Get rid of those dirty magazines and movies. Practice abstinence until you're married. Wait until you get the marriage license. After all, you could not drive a car until you got a driver's license. Even if you drove prior to getting a license, you were doing it illegally. Today, in the Spirit, I am pulling you over to say, "No license, no love!" Repeat it with me, "No license, no love!" This is even for the engaged couples. Remember God will not be mocked! (Meditate on Hebrews 13:4, I Corinthians 10:13).

Kitchen Table Reflections

1. Do you remember a time in your life where you received some devastating news that caught you off guard? Explain your answer.

2. Have you ever been to a point in your life as a Christian where the sin was so good, you ignored the warning signs from God? Feel free to share.

3. Should Christian engaged couples be participating or having sex before they say "I do?" Why or Why not?

Ingredient 6

Rude Awakening

Galatians 6:7
"Be not deceived, God is not mocked; for whatsoever a man soweth,
that shall he also reap."

We really didn't know each other all that well. We had been dating for only a few months, and suddenly I was hit with what felt like a semi-truck across the face. I can't tell my dad because I know that would be the death of me. Can't tell my friends because I'm supposed to be the "church boy," and they would never let me live it down. Can't tell my pastor…well maybe I can. Mr. Davis has been a pretty cool pastor. I have been over the youth group for a while. I have been a very faithful member at church. Man, I have talk to someone. I called Pastor Davis and I broke the news to him that I had gotten Dionne pregnant. For some reason, I think he already knew. He asked, "Do you love her?" I responded, "Yes." I had no clue what I was saying. Then he told me, "You know what you must do." Mr. Davis was very calm and it was so surprising to me. It was just what I needed. It gave me courage to know that I was not alone.

Before long, everyone knew: her parents, my parents, the church. I knew what I had done was wrong and I apologized profusely, even to Dionne. Then came the big question: "WHEN WILL YOU GET MARRIED?"

I don't know if I will marry her right away. I know that I want to marry her someday but I don't want to rush into this. Nah, I think I will wait a little bit. After all, just because we have a kid on the way does not mean we should rush into marriage. I am 28 years old and she is 30. We are so young and my dad always told me if you make a mistake, it is up to you as a man to make it right. The hardest thing for me to do was to get up in front of my congregation and apologize for having sex outside of marriage. Now that I think about it, I would never do that again because we are all sinners and if one apologizes, everyone should. On the flip side, apologizing made me a better man and shut the door on anyone who wanted to gossip further on about the matter. There is a lot of pressure and I have put others and myself in danger. God, don't leave me hanging now!

Lessons I Learned

To tell you the truth, I did not want to repent to anyone! I knew I was wrong but I just did not want to repent. I knew that I let a lot of people down but especially myself. The thing that got me to truly repent was when the people close to me did not judge me. They didn't have to. I was reaping the benefits of my own actions. I believe that the body of Christ should not condemn people because it will make them not want to repent. All of the people around me showed me love, care, and genuine concern. That's what made me repent. I pray that you show love, care, and concern to the one's you know have done wrong. That will draw them to true repentance (Meditate on Jeremiah 31:3).

Kitchen Table Reflections

1. Have you ever had to apologize in front of a large crowd of people for a mistake you made? How did you feel about that?

2. Have you ever expected someone to rake you over the coals for something you did and their response was the opposite?

Ingredient 7

Premarital Counseling

Proverbs 15:22
"Without counsel, purposes are disappointed; but in the multitude of counselors they are established."

What? Save this junk. It is irritating, invasive, and a waste of my time! I am not a "nut job" and neither is Dionne. We are both college graduates and love God. The last thing we need to be doing is putting all of our business out there for the world to see. All of these thoughts were running through my mind as my pastor and his wife counseled us. They asked all of these probing questions like, "How do you resolve conflict? Do you put the other person first before your own needs? Are you guys abstaining from sex until you actually get married? Are you all living together? When you argue, don't be so defensive. Put down your pride. The word should bring you guys back together. How well do you know your soon to be spouse? What is his/her favorite color? Ask for forgiveness and explain your intentions. What makes you angry? How will you guys spend or split holidays between the families? How much do you guys have in your savings? How is your credit?"

Looking back, I wish I had taken every question and statement very seriously. I would pay dearly for not heeding their precious words of wisdom. I wanted what I wanted and I was saved enough…so I thought. These upcoming days would test me to the very fiber of my being. To the young couple prepping for marriage, please consider these questions and many more before you actually get married. They will be the lifeline and heartbeat of your marriage. Don't be foolish like I was.

Lessons I Learned

OK. I was a straight up fool. I had already broken the cookie jar and I was just trying to make this thing legal. Though it was important, I was just trying to get through it you know? But boy, should I have listened. Had I listened in that counseling session, I could have spared my family a whole lot of pain and suffering. It is a must that as an engaged or married couple that you get counseling. If you're engaged, I would suggest at least 3 months of solid Christian counseling. For already married couples, you need to have marriage oil changes at least 3 times a year. Hook up with your local church's marriage ministry. Spend some money on the marriage seminars and outings as couples. Keep that flame of passion for one another going (Meditate on Proverbs 1:7, Proverbs 3:7, and Proverbs 13:10).

Kitchen Table Reflections

1. In your opinion, is it necessary to receive Christian marriage counseling before and after the wedding? Why or why not?

2. Define the word "Pride" in your own words. Do you see that as a constant problem in your relationship?

3. Why do a great majority of couples getting ready to get married blow off marriage counseling?

Ingredient 8

Wedding Bells

Proverbs 18:22
"Whoso findeth a wife findeth a good thing and obtaincth favor of the Lord"

At that time, I was working a job at the local casino as a surveillance off-icer. Yep, the "Eye in the Sky" sounds glamorous right? Wrong! I was in poverty, barely breaking $19,000 dollars. I was in college loan debt, I had rent to pay, car insurance, and I had my sister living with me. Her job was on and off so I did not know from week to week how all the bills were going to get paid. There was no way I was going to be ready to get married. I prayed to God very seriously that if he wanted me to marry Dionne that he needed to raise me up past $30,000. My good friend Rodney asked me about working as a manager in a very well known food chain with him. I never ever thought about working in a restaurant before, but I thought maybe it was God. I was interviewed and got it! For the 1st time in my life, I broke $30K and was on top of the world again! THANK YOU LORD!!!

Dionne and I had become closer than ever. We shared some of our deepest thoughts, hopes, and fears with each other about life. I did not have to impress her at all and she definitely did not have to impress me. All was good; however, the big question still lingered in the air about marriage. I started to think, "Would I want my child coming into a world where their

41

father and mother are not together?" That's not how I was raised. I'm going to ask her to marry me. Why not? I have stepped into the big boy arena; I must do what the big boys do.

I saved up for a ring, purchased it, and tried to figure out how to present it. Should I put it inside a cupcake or do a traditional proposal? I know! I decided to call her and act like I had been in an emergency car accident right around the corner from her house. Of course, when I called her she was frantic. I told her I would be over in an hour or so, once the police take the report, etc. Within the hour, I showed up at her door playing the pitiful just out of an accident boyfriend, and then I said it, "My whole life I waited on God to send you to me…" and I got down on one knee. As I proposed, I sang a song that my wife requires me to sing all of the time now by R&B group sensation K-Ci and Jo-Jo entitled, *All My Life*. Dionne was so surprised. She proudly said yes! We both cried tears of pure happiness. Needless to say, this was one of the happiest moments of my life.

November 13th of 2004, Hansen and Dionne Harper were wed. It was a beautiful, humbling, long, hot, tiring, stressful day. Best men, bridesmaids, pictures, family, friends…this was too much. There are three moments I remember most about our wedding: the entrance of my beautiful bride Dionne, the song *I Want You Baby*, by the ever popular Alicia Keys, that she sang to me, which made us both cry, and my smooth brother-in-law Craig. He drove us from the wedding to the reception hall blasting James Brown's *Gonna Have a Funky Good Time*. When it was all said and done, my beautiful bride and I sat back and looked at the awesomeness of God. We did it! Oh, I mean He did it! Despite all of our fears, distractions, trials, and tribulations, the Lord kept us. Would we live happily ever after? I don't know, but at that time I knew I had my God, my girl, and my gig. GGG. What more did I need?

Lessons I Learned

I just can't imagine not having done the right thing by marrying Dionne. I will admit that I did have second thoughts, but I couldn't let our baby come into the world without his parents being together. To me, at least, that would have the baby confused. My parents did not bring me up that way, so I was not going to do that to my son. I was going to marry Dionne whether she had gotten pregnant or not, but I never expected to do it that soon. Maybe you are in the same situation. Pray about it. Most of the time, the answer is right in front of your face. When we finally got married, we were so optimistic, bright eyed, but we did not know anything. Our wedding and reception were nice but I realized that the wedding was really for everyone else. When it was all over, Dionne and I were so relieved that we just fell out in the hotel room. Were we ready for what we had done? Probably not but we enjoyed the big day anyway. You'll have even bigger decisions to make after you are married. Believe that! Marriage is not the end; it is just the beginning.

Kitchen Table Reflections

1. Take a real close look at your life. Are you really prepared for a God-centered marriage?

2. Name at least 3 successful marriages that you have seen in your lifetime. What was so good about them?

3. MEN: How did/would you propose to your wife/fiance'? WOMEN: How did/would you like your husband/fiance' to propose to you?

4. In your opinion, is marriage the answer to all of your problems and worries? Why or why not?

Ingredient 9

BaggageClaims:
His & Hers

2 Corinthians 10:5
"Casting down arguments and every high thing that exalts itself against the knowledge of God, bringing every thought into captivity to the obedience of Christ."

Have you ever gone on vacation with just a couple bags but on your return home, you have what seems to be a thousand bags. You start to wonder to yourself, "Where did all this stuff come from?" That's just how marriage is. You start out with your little stuff, but combined with the other person's stuff it tends to be baggage overload if not properly handled. Oh, everyone brings some baggage to the table. Whether they claim it or not, it is between you, them, and God. After the wedding, all of the lovey-dovey stuff started to wear off and we began to slowly get on each other's last nerve! This part of our marriage is called *Baggage Claim* because I was carrying bags and she was as well. I finally started to realize that we came from two totally different worlds. Go ahead and laugh before you read this next part because I know you guys will be able to see something you identify with.

His

I grew up in a house of married parents. My father and mother ran a loving home. My dad ran most of the business affairs, such as paying bills, and my mother was a homemaker most of my life. She then became a teacher during my teen years. My dad protected my mom from a lot of things. In ways I believed he sheltered her so much that she was scared to make a decision without him actually being around. My dad provided for 3 boys (including myself) and 1 girl; he showed us that a real man was someone who loved God, took care of his family, went to work, and stayed out of trouble. My parents discussed just about everything. My siblings and I could not get away with much of anything. If we asked my dad for something, he would ask what my mother said, and vice versa. We did not have everything we wanted, but both my parents worked to get us what we needed. I was always an outspoken person. If something happened, I would either tell it or be a part of it. I wanted to go do it and not talk about it. My father would always say, "Boy, why don't you sit down somewhere? Stop asking so many questions!"

I came into this marriage assuring myself that the strong personality in my wife would not rule me. "She may try that on somebody else but not me," I'd say. I was going to show her what a real man was. In my family, the man was the head of the household. People could suggest what they wanted, but my dad had the final say so. Coming into our marriage, I had to cut the thinking process that I always had to have the final say because that was the beginning of so many of our arguments.

Hers

Dionne grew up as the child of divorced parents. She lived with her mother the majority of the time and visited her father on the weekends. As a young girl, she watched her mom run the household and work; she did both very well. Dionne brought her understanding of a woman's role in a divorced home into her married home. Her mom did it all (bills, feeding, clothing, nurturing, etc.) because she HAD to. In our household, Dionne had to learn to discuss problems, bills, and allotment of monies with me. That was something she never saw. Therefore, it was something she had to learn to do with me.

We both came into our marriage thinking we knew what was best for ourselves and the other person. Dionne had to release the idea that she knew it all. By holding on to that belief, she was not listening to or valuing any of my ideas and opinions. By releasing the idea that her opinions were always the best, we were able to listen to each other's opinions and feelings and come to a compromise. Sometimes we would use my ideas, while other times we would use hers.

Dionne has always been one that thought before she spoke. Often times her thoughts and feelings stayed with her because she felt that they were her personal prized possessions. She did not like sharing her feelings with anybody but God. The more I would try to discuss something with her, the more she would shut down. I hated that. All in all, the contents of our bags were being emptied daily. My wife and I were just trying to make sure that our garbage was outside on the curb so that God, our garbage man, wouldn't pass it by.

Lessons I Learned

Congratulations. If you have made it this far in the book, surely, some of this information has struck a chord with you and your mate. Being married, we must shake off the tendency to collect baggage, old or new, daily. We must sit down as a couple every day and be able to be open about differences in opinions concerning our childhood experiences as well as our daily routines. Past and present experiences form the basis for how we deal with our baggage issues. The majority of the baggage comes from the differing ideologies of how you both were raised. In your family, the father may have been the homemaker. In her family, the mother may have been the breadwinner. It all depends. You as a couple must come up with how YOUR family will do things. You are a new creation in Christ so what worked when you were single will not work now.

The other portion of baggage just comes from normal day to day routines you establish as a couple. Daily baggage may come from constant pressure from your professions, bosses, coworkers, extended family, kids, or maybe even your own spouse. We must determine as a Godly married couple that we will not create or accept baggage build up. I know at our house, by the time we finally did get together at night, we were definitely not communicating. We were professional bag collectors heaping stories of baggage and sadness on each other. By the time we both laid down, we were both smothered in it.

There is great news, though! Jesus specializes in baggage elimination. Look at what he did for us on Cavalry's cross. He collected all of our baggage and bore it on himself so that we would not have to (Isaiah 53:5). Marriage should be the most fulfilling union in the world because our baggage is eliminated. Don't burden down what God has created with the filth that the devil tries to heap on your relationship. Confess with me: I will not create or accept baggage build up in my relationship! Say it again like you believe it: I will not create or accept baggage build up in this house! Our God specializes in baggage elimination. You have a long journey ahead of you, so eliminate the bags, alleviate the stress, and uplift the name of the Lord Jesus Christ in your relationship.

Kitchen Table Reflections

1. List three bags that each of you brought into your current relationship.

2. Are you personally willing to work through these issues and let go of the bags? What about your spouse? Talk about this topic one-on-one over dinner.

Ingredient 10

Brace Yourself

Psalms 127:1
"Except the Lord build the house, they labor in vain that build it: except the Lord keep the city, the watchman waketh in vain."

Just about the time I started working good, we needed a home before the baby came. We applied for our first home in Hammond, Indiana and we got it! Yep, first time homeowners, every man's dream. Dionne was about 8 months pregnant. One month later at Michael Reese Hospital in Chicago, IL at 10 a.m., January 10, 2005 my son Zion Caleb Harper was born. I was on cloud 1 million! I knew exactly how I wanted to raise my son. Therein lay one of the problems in our new marriage; Dionne knew exactly how she wanted to raise our son, too. Somebody had to be right. Somebody had to be wrong. The first 2 years of our marriage were decent, but then, all of a sudden, the rug started to slide right from under us.

First, I was still the newest manager of my restaurant at that time, so I was working upward of 80 plus hours a week. I was never home. Dionne was doing her student teaching in Illinois but she was not getting paid. Not cool! Our son Zion spent most of the time in daycare, which I knew my wife and I despised, but we were on that paper chase.

Thanksgiving, I was working. Christmas, I was working. Sunday, I was working. Mother's Day, Father's Day, Easter, you name it; I worked them all. As a restaurant manager, I especially hated swing shifts from 3 p.m. to midnight. Dionne basically ran the household and she treated me as such. We had thousands of arguments where I felt like we were not even married to each other, from arguments on how Zion should be dressed to how much sex was too much. I remember one day Dionne accused me of being a sex maniac. I, in turn, told her that I could only be a maniac if I got some more than twice a month! We fought over whose parents' house to go to for the holidays, if I was off work that is. It truly was a terrible time. We fought both verbally and physically like cats and dogs. When our parents showed up on the scene, they decided to be neutral and stay out of our mess. As a matter of fact, neither of our parents ever took sides. If anything, they were hard on the both of us. That is why I love both of our parents. Despite that small positive, our relationship didn't get any better. Needless to say, there was no, happily ever after for us. The better phrase for our marriage was "happily ever never." The only thing we did do right was go to church. But eventually, we ended up arguing about that, too.

In order to provide for the family, I spent countless hours at the job, not because I wanted to, but because I felt I had to. I was important at work and people seemed to need and appreciate me. I excelled as a restaurant manager. I received dozens of awards at my job; I was a superstar in the workplace but the invisible man at home. It hurt my heart to come home from a hard day's work to find out that my son Zion, who was about 3 years old at that time, did not even want to come to me because he barely saw me. Zion thought I was a stranger. All that I was doing was for him and my wife, and even they did not want to put up with me. My marriage was up and down for two and a half years. When year three came around, only God could save me from the fiery darts that we were getting ready to come at our relationship! "God, I am a man!" is something I said often to God, "I get treated better in the streets than I do at home!" I felt strongly that I had made a mistake. Every type of thought stormed through my head: thoughts of taking off, ending my life, ending our marriage. I often asked God, "Where are you? I heard and saw you while I was a boy, but I am a man now. I have BIG problems, and you seem to be nowhere around. If you are real, show me. If not, I'll do what I want to do. Lift me up God, or let me die!"

Lessons I Learned

Everything was so crazy at this time. I was working hard and long hours, and I was still in a very new marriage. Without the grace and mercy of God, I know my marriage would have failed! One thing that I have realized is that it doesn't matter what you gain and achieve outside the home, if you lose your family in the process, it is never worth it. An elder named James Middleton in our former church shared a dream that he had with me. In this dream he died and went to heaven and God asked him, "Where is the rest of you?" James asked, "God, what are you talking about? I am here. I made it!" God asked him one more time, "Where is the rest of you?" As James looked dumbfounded, God replied, "Where are your wife and kids? You left them behind. You must leave Heaven and return no more!" God views my family and I as one. Isn't that something? After hearing this dream, I was convinced that I would never put anything above my family other than God! Especially in times of frustration, we must still lean on and trust in the everlasting and loving arms of Christ!

Kitchen Table Reflections

1. What is the importance of really getting to know each other before you get married?

2. Have you ever worked so many hours at the job that your kid(s) did not even recognize who you were?

3. Do you ever feel that you are a "superstar" at work, and the "invisible man/woman" at home to your spouse? Explain your answer.

4. Do your in-laws take you or your spouse's side during arguments, or do they deal an even hand in counseling you both as a couple?

5. Have you ever contemplated ending your marriage? Why or why not?

Ingredient 11

Restore My Soul

Proverbs 16:18
"Pride goes before destruction and a haughty spirit before a fall."

It was just a normal dysfunctional evening at the Harper household and Dionne asked if she could talk to me. Oh, boy! What is it now? Dionne went on to ask if her sister and her husband could come stay with us until they got on their feet. She said that we could use the money, and we did need it. I was for it as long as it was for a short period. After all, if we were in need I would want someone to help us out. They moved in, and they drove me crazy. I know I drove them crazy, too. By this time, I had switched from working at the restaurant to being a full time 8th grade teacher. I went to work and came home early, but I always came with a lot of homework to grade. By this time my wife was teaching as well ,and it was terrible. We constantly had a clash of minds, of standards, and of household matters. Dionne was just trying to keep the peace. On top of that, remember, I was already an absentee dad and husband. I then turned into an absentee landlord. I couldn't take it; this was going to drive more space between my wife and I…so I thought.

One weekend, when my brother and sister-in-law were gone, Dionne said something to me out of the blue. Whatever it was, I thought it was so disrespectful that I flipped out. To this day, I still can't remember what she said, but it was the last straw! I forgot what my response was, but it was not Christian. I verbally tried to hurt her for what she had said to me. Everything became a blur, and before I knew it the local police department was outside our home. With lights flashing, my mind went back to how I had left the restaurant business to begin a teaching career. Dionne had just gotten licensed as a teacher. Anyway, my mind was back to the flashing light and my eyes floated over to my son Zion screaming at the top of his 3 year old lungs. This did not even seem real; it was like a warped episode of *CSI*. Dionne ran outside like I had beaten her down to the ground, the neighbors were looking, and Zion was crying. In all of this time, the officer had not said a word. The officer finally asked Dionne what happened, and she went on and on about what she claimed I did.

By now, I am just outside dazed like, "What? This really can't be happening to me, could it? Where did all of this come from? I would rather be anywhere but here, God!" The officer finally got around to asking me what happened, and I clearly told him that everything was over exaggerated. I did not touch Dionne. All of a sudden I saw my parents show up and I could not have been happier; I had called them earlier just in case I went to jail. The officer shouted to the both of us, "Now both of y'all shut up!" He asked us what our professions were. We told him that we were teachers. The officer looked as if he was going slap us both across our faces. He asked, "Teachers?" as if we were supposed to be above problems. What the officer said next is something I never forgot, "If I take you both to jail, which is what both of you deserve, your son will be put in FOSTER CARE. Now if I have to be called back over to this house again, you are both going to jail and your son is going to be a ward of the state. Understand?"

Man, Dionne and I were embarrassed and startled at the same time. The officer was exactly right. All of our foolishness was going to get our son taken away from us, which I would never wish on any marriage. I know you're thinking we learned our lesson after that, right? WRONG!!

The rollercoaster tracks only go down from here; the story only gets worse. My brother and sister-in-law stayed longer than expected, the teaching thing was shaky at best, our relationship was basically down the tubes, and the church had me running doing this and that. "AHHHHH" I cried out, "God SAVE ME! I AM GOING CRAZY! I AM TIRED OF ALL OF THIS! THIS IS NOT WHAT I ASKED YOU FOR!" It was all hopeless, and I truly didn't care anymore.

A few months later, I was at home looking at the game or something on television, and Dionne said something cutting at me. I lost it again! This time I got in her face and let her know that I was not to be trampled on like a piece of trash. I was a man. Before I knew it, my brother-in-law ran in like Neo from *The Matrix* to save me from Dionne. I was so angry that I didn't even realize Dionne had gone into the kitchen and brought back a butcher knife. She was actually going to stab me! Here's the miracle: my brother-in-law was not even supposed to be home. He hadn't left because he couldn't find his keys. While looking for them, he heard us going at it upstairs and came running. My brother-in-law grabbed her hand just as she lunged forward to stab me in the chest. God allowed my brother-in-law to save my life! But after all this drama, I did not think my marriage could be saved. I was going to be OUT! This was no "Relationship." This was a "Wrecklationship" and it is not for me. We went our separate ways for 3 whole days. I should have been feeling good with her gone, but instead I felt so low. The house was empty, just me and my thoughts.

Lessons I Learned

This was hands down the worst day of my life. Knives, police cars, my son crying, almost being taken to jail...I had enough! At this point, I really believed that I had made a mistake by marrying Dionne. We were just too different. The truth is, it should have never gotten to that point. Our communication by that time had totally broken down. Our trust for each other was non-existent. Ephesians 5:25 says that I was to love my wife as Christ loved the Church and give myself to her. Dionne was making it very hard though. Further down in verse 28 it says that we are to love our wives as our own bodies and he that loveth his wife loveth himself.

As I remembered scuffling and arguing with my wife, I realized that I did not love myself. After Dionne almost took my life, it made me realize that the show of violence was just pride in disguise. No one wanted to admit that the other person was right, and sometimes we would just plain ignore the other person's feelings all together. Thank God he sends those guardian angels right in time to protect you from yourself. I know now that my wife is just as and really more important than myself. I will never venture back to that dark moment in our marriage ever again. The next time an argument comes up and you feel that violence and pride rising up, just go back and remember how many times you have made a mess of things before God. Remember how many times God has looked over your mess. Realize that your spouse is fragile and he/she is the best and most important investment you have other than Christ. Participate in daily prayers early in the morning and at night together. That way you can start and end the day with God. I'm telling you, just watch the arguments die down.

Kitchen Table Reflections

1. Has dysfunction become a normal part of your family? How will you aim to change that?

2. Do you have a "Wrecklationship" or a relationship? What is the difference?

3. Is it possible for you and your mate to go back to the original time when you were married? Look at pictures, videotapes, DVDs; drive back by the church or reception hall. Set this up as a date night without the kids.

4. Is winning the argument between you and your spouse more important than peace in your home? Ask yourself, what is more important, being right or being married?

Ingredient 12

The Idiot Light

Proverbs 3:35
"The wise shall inherit glory: But shame shall be the promotion of fools."

Some old man somewhere once said that if a light comes on on your car's dashboard for the brakes or engine, those are what they call the "idiot lights". You're driving a car that is in need of maintenance; so if your car breaks down, it's your fault because you were warned. Well it is apparently self-evident that my "idiot light" has been on forever, and I have just been ignoring the signs. Breakdown? My relationship and life were both broke down to the ground. Yep, I thought everything was about over until one day something strange happened.

Donna and Craig, my brother and sister-in-law who are saved and were the youth pastors at their church, invited Dionne and I to this Christian marriage counseling session. Oh, here we go again with this counseling stuff. I was ready to hear a little bit more because I obviously failed miserably at my relationship. I asked Dionne if she wanted to go but she said no. Finally, at the last minute she changed her mind and went anyway.

Yep, this is awkward. We went to this session unoptimistic, sort of irritated, and seriously hoping this was not a waste of our time. The other young couples there were so loving, nice, and treated us like we were family. We talked about a whole lot of things that night but the one thing that changed our marriage forever is what the facilitator had us do. She gave us each a 3 by 5 note card and told us to write down what animal we thought the other one was during a heated argument, but we were not to let our significant other see what we wrote down. I was like, "Cool. This is my turn to really tear into Dionne." One guy turned his card over and said that his wife was a woodpecker because she just would not leave him alone. She just kept on pecking away at him for the smallest things. His wife drew him as a lightning bug, because he only lit up at night when he wanted some sex. Oh, it was on and poppin! Of course, I couldn't wait until our turn came around because I was about to jump this party off. From all of the ways and times I have been disrespected and talked down to, Dionne would feel my wrath! Snakes, gophers, lions, tigers, electric eels…one can only imagine the descriptions that were put into the atmosphere that night.

Finally, our turn came around and Dionne went first. I just knew that she would call me something cute like a lion or a bear. The card was flipped over and it said bull. A bull? Seriously? The other couples were silent but very attentive. OK…I got you; it's my turn now. I didn't even wait to be prompted to turn my card over. I flipped my card over and it said rhinoceros. This floored all the couples at the session because the majority of the couples had little cute descriptions like fireflies, rabbits, cats, etc. When the leader saw the BULL vs. RHINO, he seemed really concerned. The counselor said out of all the couples they had mentored over the years, this is the most dangerous combination they had ever seen. At this point, no one was moving, talking, or laughing in the room. They said that both animals are big and strong. More dangerously, both have very shap horns and upon impact, we were either going to hurt/kill each other or an innocent bystander.

At that moment I had an epiphany. My mind immediately rushed back to seeing my son outside in the cold crying, the police giving us a warning, my wife enraged with a butcher knife aimed to stab me…somebody was going to get hurt but not while I was still alive! Thank you God for waking me up! If I were to succeed as a husband, father, provider, and man of God, I would have to start putting down my selfish pride and start giving more to my family. I needed to give more time, more love, and show more patience. God, I want my house to be a resort for love instead of a hotel of resentment. It does not matter what she does. It matters what I do!

As for the aspect of thinking too many people were in my business, I finally realized that my brother and sister-in-law were not in my business. God placed them in my life because they were about God's business for both me and Dionne. I would like to personally thank Pastor Craig and Donna Barnett (my brother and sister-in-law). By our small sacrifice of letting them stay in our home, and by their big sacrifice of putting up with us, they ended up being an integral part (along with our parents Floyd and Ovellia Harper and Ruby Douglas) of saving our marriage and saving us. Just this past Christmas I had to apologize openly to my brother and sister-in-law about my attitude towards them at that time. God allowed all of these names mentioned to save our marriage from self-destruction. Thank you Lord for the unexpected helpers you send our way all of the time. I thought it was over, and You proved me wrong.

Lessons I Learned

I tried to blame all of my life's woes and sorrows on everybody but myself. Though I felt alone, God was always there. God brought my brother and sister-in-law into our lives, along with my parents and Dionne's mother, to save our marriage. If the devil had his way, our marriage would've ended up in disaster. An outsider looking in may have even said we should get divorced because of all the dysfunction. My challenge to married couples is that if your relationship is on the rocks, find someone who has a strong couple's ministry. After that, sign up for whatever they have going on. I'm telling you, it will become the life or death of your relationship. Remember, many more people suffer in a divorce than just the man and wife. Your kids, co-workers, fellow parishioners, friends, and family suffer because they are a part of each of you. Take the time to use the 3 by 5 cards that I have in the discussion part of this section. I am telling you, using this tool was one of the biggest game changers in my marriage. It works, guys! It works.

Kitchen Table Reflections

1. Take the time as a couple to list three "idiot lights" that are on currently in your relationship. Take 3 minutes to discuss them with your spouse or another couple.

2. Take about 15 minutes. Get some 3 by 5 note cards. On them, describe a type of animal your spouse/fiancé portrays when they get angry. (Remember, you are not to let them look at your cards until the moderator asks you to flip them over, one person at a time and please, no fighting. This should be very fun.)

3. Imagine if those two animals on your 3 by 5 crashed head on into each other? What did the Lord impress upon your heart when you imagined that?

4. Name at least 5 changes you each should make in response to the reading of this chapter for the sake of your marriage. Be fair and sensible. (Share these 5 things with each other over a meal…No kids allowed!)

5. Pray to God right now that he would help you both to understand the hurt that the other is experiencing and ask him to show you how to respond to it in a positive and effective way.

Ingredient 13

W.I.P.D.

Isaiah 54:8
"But now, O Lord thou art our father; we are the clay, and thou our potter; and we all are the work of thy hand."

During my days as a young man, I was so concerned about my reputation. The friends I used to hang around often said if you started rambling on about your girlfriend too much, or if you were always complaining about how your girlfriend mistreated or played you, "Man, she got you Whipped!" I remember that burned me up inside because the last thing I wanted for anyone to think that I was a punk and a softy. Do any of you remember being called whipped by your peers?

Nowadays, I think about how God miraculously brought Dionne and I out of the situations that we went through to enhance our marriage. I can truly announce to you that I am officially WIPD! Go ahead and say it. I promise I won't get mad.

By now, I already know that you couples are asking the question, "Why would I want to get WIPD? What is WIPD anyway, and when can this process happen to our marriage?" Let me ask you guys a hypothetical question. If someone you did not know gave you the key to a lockbox you knew had $1 million in it, how quick would you use that key? Pretty fast right? Let's be serious. Some of you are just enduring your marriage, and that is not what God wants. Marriage is not a punishment. It's a gift. God wants you to unlock that treasure he has given you in your husband or wife. Funny thing about a gift, what you pass up, somebody else will think they won the lottery. You have hit a critical point in your marriage. You can't afford to mess this up. Don't you want to have a successful and thriving marriage? Aren't you tired of all the fights and miscommunication?

God has revealed to me the WIPD process for couples. There are four simple steps to maintaining a successful and God-centered marriage. Worship..... Intimacy.....Prayer.....and Dedication. These are 4 sure fire ways that Dionne and I have used over the years to aggressively defend our covenant before God. Are we perfect? No! However, I wish the WIPD method was around when we were going through our turmoil. The real reason for me sharing my life experience with you and writing this book is to prevent couples all over the world from making the same stupid mistakes we made in our marriage. If your marriage is in trouble, at a standstill, or thriving, the WIPD method will work for you. After using the WIPD method in your marriage, I guarantee you will begin to develop and see your spouse as an asset, not an enemy. Let's get WIPD!

Worship

According to the Webster dictionary, the word worship means, "to regard with great or extravagant respect, honor, or devotion." If you really want to enrich your marriage you must:

Worship God Together Every Morning

Psalms 95:6 says, "O come, let us worship and bow down; let us kneel before the Lord our maker." When you both start trying to do this faithfully, of course, the devil will try to make you sleepier than ever, but press your way. Your marital breakthrough is right within your reach! Worshiping God together not only strengthens the bond between you and God, but it tightens up your bond with your mate. Before, Dionne and I wouldn't pray in the morning at all, and we usually would have a defeated day. However, since we have been doing this faithfully, God has blessed us to the point where we race to pray in the morning. You can do the same and believe me; you will see the fruit of your results immediately if you stick with it.

In addition, when you and your spouse worship the Lord God togther you become a powerful weapon. When you all just buckle down and start giving the Lord all the praise and all the glory, no devil in hell will be able to stop your progress. While writing this book, God gave me a bow and arrow illustration that should help you out a lot. Have you ever seen someone pick up an arrow and throw it at the target? Have you ever seen someone taking the bow alone and throwing it at the target? Probably not! Separately they are pretty ineffective, but together they are a force to be reckoned with. You can hit any target now because you are working together (Matthew 4:4 2 Corinthians 10:4) .That is what worship with your spouse every morning can do for you marriage. Are you ready to hit the target? Take about 10 minutes each morning to start off with prayer, a worship song, and a scripture for the next 2 weeks. Make worshiping God a habit, and you will create an atmosphere of victory in your marriage!

Intimacy

The word intimacy means, "Close or warm friendship or understanding/relationship." -Webster.

Psalms 63:1-8
"O God, thou art my God; early will I seek thee: my soul thirsteth for thee, my flesh longeth for thee in a dry and thirsty land, where no water is; To see thy power and thy glory, so as I have seen thee in the sanctuary. Because thy loving kindness is better than life, my lips shall praise thee. Thus will I bless thee while I live: I will lift up my hands in thy name. My soul shall be satisfied as with marrow and fatness; and my mouth shall praise thee with joyful lips: When I remember thee upon my bed, and meditate on thee in the night watches. Because thou hast been my help, therefore in the shadow of thy wings will I rejoice. My soul followeth hard after thee: thy right hand upholdeth me."

Be Intimate with God

I think about David in Psalms 63:1-8. David talks about having a father/son relationship with God. David constantly reminds God of his deep need for him. That's intimacy at it's finest. Now both of you throughout the whole day, just began to adore and love on God like how David did in Psalms 63:1-8. Once you do this daily, you will be on your way to a more intimate time as a couple.

Be Intimate with Each Other

Early in my marriage, I really thought I was intimate with Dionne. And ladies for men, that means that we are having good, fun loving sex every night. On the other hand, Dionne wanted me to cuddle, talk, and whisper our wedding song to her in her ears. We were both irritating each other. It wasn't until very late in our marriage we found that we both were missing the point. If we ever were going to last within the institution of marriage we needed to stop being so formal with each other as couples. I told Dionne one day that I felt as if we treated each other as business partners. She agreed.

To break up the monotony, we started focusing on each other. Do you all have a pet name for each other? Take about 30 seconds to just call your spouse by their pet name. If you don't have a pet name pick one right now. You see, that's intimate. Start dating each other again. Laugh with each other a lot. Express your feelings to each other calmly without prejudice. As for sex, your bedroom should be a sensual Olympic event where both of you win the GOLD. Aim for both to be satisfied. Hey it's OK! You're married. Read Hebrews 13:4. Don't deprive your spouse. Make your spouse a priority. Intimacy is a choice. Choose Godly intimacy and watch your marriage skyrocket!

Prayer

The word prayer means, "An act of communion with God, a god, or another object of worship, such as in devotion, confession, praise, or thanksgiving." –Free Dictionary.com.

Honestly, how many of us communicate clearly with our spouse everyday? How about God? We're all probably guilty of not doing such a great job. If your marriage is going to work, you must experience clear communcation between God and each other. Before you can communcate clearly to God or your spouse you must:

Pray Against Unforgiveness

Unforgiveness is the #1 reason why couples' prayers don't get answered. This is also a nucleus for confusion in the home. Have you and your wife ever had an argument early in the morning and you just went straight out of the house to work? How did your day go? For us it was terrible. That is why Ephesians 4:26-27 says that, "When angry, do not sin; do not ever let your wrath (your exasperation, your fury, indignation) last until the sun goes down. Leave no (such room or foothold for the devil. Give no opportunity to him. God promises that he will not hear your prayer if you do not forgive each other (Mark 11:25). So if you both are looking for a real breakthrough, GET UP...GET OVER IT......and Get YOUR PRAYER ON!!

Pray the Word

Daily my son and daughter remind me and my wife of the promises we made to them. As of lately, my younger daughter Zoe is fascinated with Chuck E. Cheese. One day, we told her that we were going to take her there Sunday, but it was only Wednesday. Until we actually stepped into Chuck E. Cheese that Sunday, she continued to ask us if we were going every second of every day. What persistence! What was she really doing? She was just reminding us of what we had promised. That's all prayer is, reminding God of what He promised from what He said in His word. What has God promised to you and your marriage? God is only obligated to His word, and He has placed His word above His name (Psalms 138:2). Just like my little daughter, petition God for your requests and expect the results (Read Matthew 18:19-20).

Don't Judge Judy, Judge Mathis

I hate to admit this, but there was a time in my marriage where I would judge my wife's prayer. Isn't that ridiculous? Usually, there is one that thinks they are more grounded in the word than the other. Jesus never said that your prayers should be short or long, but isn't it funny how when we try to be God. It goes terribly wrong every time. Husbands, turn to your wife and say, "Hello Judge Judy!" Wives turn to your husbands and say, "Hello, Judge Mathis!" Stop judging everything like you are the final authority on prayer. Prayer is not a competition. It is an admission by both parties of your desperate need for God's guidance. For instance, my wife would say a short prayer like, "God, just thank you for this day." In my mind I was like," Let me show her how it's really done!" I would go on and on trying to show her up. Have you and your spouse ever had this battle? Prayer is a team event as it pertains to your marriage. If you are doing what I did, stop it. It is dividing not only your marriage but your household as well. This is a verse that helped me (Matthew 6:7). Remember, it is not the length of your prayer, it is the strength of your prayer…together!

Dedication

The act of dedicating means to "bind yourself (intellectually or emotionally) to a course of action."
–Free Dictionary.com.

Psalms 42:1
"As a deer panteth for the water so my soul longeth after thee."

Dedication to God: Unconditional Love

What was David actually getting at? David knew that just like the deer, he was totally dependant on God's supply. The deer has nothing significant he has created himself. The deer is totally reliant on God for water, food, and shelter but the deer is not lazy either. The deer wakes up everyday searching for provision and is dedicated to doing so. How much more are we? You and your spouse should be dedicated to the things of God. Wake up every morning searching for God because He is literally your only source and supply. Some practical ways of doing this is to go to church, have devotion during the week, donating time and money to Godly causes, die to yourself and live for God. It is my prayer that your marriages begin to have, "Deer-like Dedication." Watch how your marriage grows through the roof.

Dedication to Spouse: Unconditional Love

Luke 12:34 (NIV)
"For where your treasure is, there your heart will be also."

I remember when my wife and I first got married. Boy, you couldn't tell us anything. I wanted to be around her every waking moment. She wanted to be around me all the time, too. Everything was an adventure and it was us against the world. As time went on, kids, jobs, and differences of opinions started the cycle of not being dedicated to each other like we should. It is so easy to do, isn't it? But I am am telling you, the worst mistake you can make is to not show that you are dedicated to your spouse daily. Here are some surefire ways to make sure your spouse feels that you are dedicated.

Get together just because. Go to the park or your favorite restaurant. Play a board game. Put the kids to sleep early to watch your favorite movie. Choose to be with your spouse! You must put each other first in your lives.

Block out a couple of hours each day for some time together. Spend as much time with your wife as you do with your cell phone, iPad, or Kindle. Instead of Facebooking friends, go look your spouse in the face and tell them you love them. Will you let technology ruin your marriage? Newsflash…you did not get married to Microsoft or Samsung. You got married to _____. Would you rather for the battery in your phone to die or for the battery of your relationship to die? Get a clue. Be dedicated.

Lessons I Learned

Can you believe my journey? I went from begging God to get me married then a few years later begging him to get me out of a marriage. You see, for so long I was trying to do it on my own, tune myself up, and make my own way. Without fail, every time I have tried things my way, it ends in sheer tragedy. You've read my story. I have now learned to just rest in the process. He is responsible for the success of our process. I am happy to say that my marriage with Dionne is better than ever. I am a better Father to Zion and Zoe. God had me to write this book to help other struggling married couples along in their journey. I don't have all of the answers. However I can point you to the master that does…God. Marriage is a life-long process. It is not a 50-yard dash!

As I look back over the last 8 years, there were minutes, hours, and days where I felt totally hopeless. Even as I heard Bible scriptures at different points in my life, it did nothing for me. I really just wanted God to take me away from here. Now I realize that God is the smartest, wisest, most intelligent, awesome, and loving being there is. Jeremiah 29:11 said that He knows the thoughts He thinks of us. They are thoughts of good and not of evil. Once we know and understand that all of the ingredients in our lives are not bad, our marriage can just rest in God's mixing bowl. He will do the adding, stirring, beating, and mixing. You may wonder at times how you will make it through, but in the end your marriage will become the marvelous masterpiece God originally designed it to be.

Nowadays, I think about how God has brought Dionne and I out of the situations we went through so we can help your marriage. I can truly announce to you that our marriage is officially WIPD! Dionne and I are still happily married. We just celebrated our 8-year anniversary. I am a 9th grade World History teacher, author, and minister. Dionne recently went back to work as a 7th/8th grade Science teacher. God blessed us so that Dionne was able to be a stay-at-home mom and really invest extra time into our kids. Isn't God good? Our son Zion just turned 8 on January 10th and is as smart as I don't know what. He gets straight As in school, and loves basketball and Jesus Christ dearly. I am so glad that the devil did not get the victory 4 years ago when Dionne and I had him out there with all that police foolishness. Oh, I forgot to mention that we have a new edition to the family now: Zoe Liberty Harper, our little girl. She was born on August 12th, 2010. Zoe is a firecracker and won't sit still for a minute.

If you enjoyed this book, pass it on to at least five married couples who have been struggling or who just want to do a maintenance check on their marriage. After reading this book, if you notice another couple that seems to have things going south in their marriage I want you to promise me that the first thing you will do is tell them that they need to "GO GET WIPD!" May God bless your marriage forever in Jesus Name….Amen!!

Kitchen Table Reflections

1. Looking over your life, name some ingredients on your journey that God has *W.I.P.D.* together to make you a better person.

2. In your own words, take a few minutes to write down the top 5 qualities you love about your mate. Now write down at least 5 opportunities that your mate can improve on. Fold it up, go to dinner, and discuss them. Believe me. It works! No kids!

3. God gave me a diagram to bless your marriage or engagement. *The W.I.P.D. Defeated Diagram* (p.77) shows a couple just getting married, but after that they start going their own ways. The more a couple gets away from God, the further they get away from their partner. Then finally, they end up getting overwhelmed and in divorce court. However, *The W.I.P.D. Victory Diagram* shows that same couple getting married, but as they walk forward together toward God, they enter God's protection zone. The cares of life and divorce court can't tear them apart because they are protected by God. Use the tips in this book to keep your marriage on the path to victory.

For more companion resources, visit us at www.gotwipd.com.

The W.I.P.D. Defeated Diagram

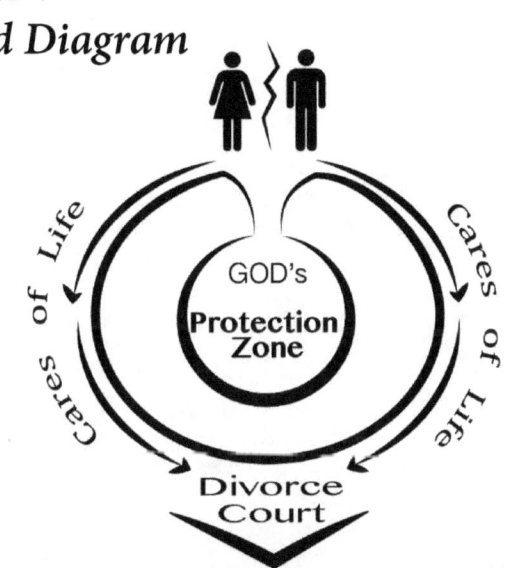

The W.I.P.D. Victory Diagram

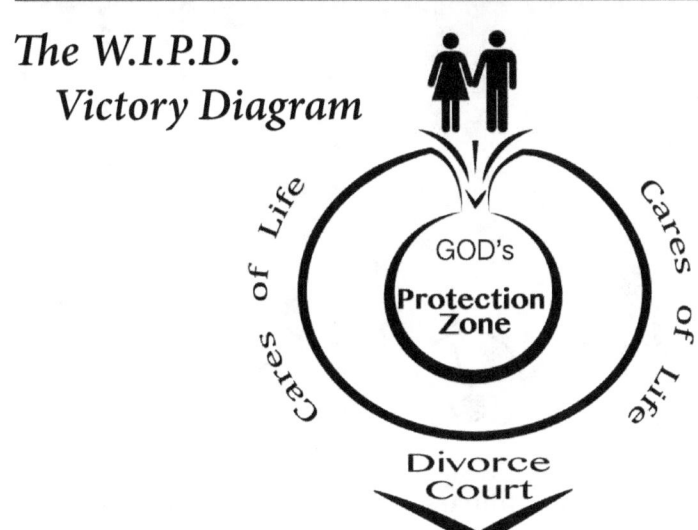

Hansen Harper is available for seminars, workshops, and book signings.
Contact Hansen Harper at:
www.gotwipd.com